RAINBOW magic ®

The Pet Keeper Fairies

For Kate Granlund, with lots of love

Special thanks to
Sue Mongredien

ORCHARD BOOKS
338 Euston Road, London NW1 3BH
Orchard Books
Hachette Children's Books
Level 17/207 Kent Street, Sydney, NSW 2000
A Paperback Original

First published in Great Britain in 2006
Rainbow Magic is a registered trademark of Working Partners Limited.
Series created by Working Partners Limited, London W6 OQT

Text © Working Partners Limited 2006
Illustrations © Georgie Ripper 2006
The right of Georgie Ripper to be identified as the illustrator
of this work has been asserted by her in accordance
with the Copyright, Designs and Patents Act, 1988.
A CIP catalogue record for this book is available
from the British Library.

ISBN 1 84616 166 5
1 3 5 7 9 10 8 6 4 2

Printed and bound in China

Katie the Kitten Fairy

by Daisy Meadows

illustrated by Georgie Ripper

ORCHARD BOOKS

www.rainbowmagic.co.uk

Fairies with their pets I see
And yet no pet has chosen me!
So I will get some of my own
To share my perfect frosty home.

This spell I cast. Its aim is clear:
To bring the magic pets straight here.
Pet Keeper Fairies soon will see
Their seven pets living with me!

Contents

A Very Unusual Kitten

"Catch!"

Kirsty Tate hurled a tennis ball into the air and watched as her friend Rachel Walker ran across the grass to catch it. It was the first day of the Easter holidays and Rachel had come to stay with Kirsty's family for a whole week. The two girls were in the park

while Kirsty's parents were at the supermarket. With the sun shining brightly and no trace of a cloud in the sky, it felt like perfect holiday weather.

Rachel held up the ball triumphantly. "Your turn," she called. "Ready?"

Before Kirsty could reply, there was a loud sound of barking, and both girls spun around to see a large black dog thundering past them.

Rachel jumped back
quickly as the dog
raced by. "Is that
a squirrel it's
chasing?" she asked,
staring after it.

Kirsty shielded her
eyes from the sun for
a better look. "No, it's a kitten!" she
exclaimed. Her eyebrows shot up in
surprise at the sight of the tiny white
and grey kitten scrambling across the
grass as fast as its little legs could
carry it. "What's a kitten
doing in the park?"

"I don't know – but
that dog's about to
catch it," Rachel said
in alarm. "Come on!"

The two girls started to run after the animals. But before they'd got very far there was a sudden flash of bright light, and then a cloud of amber sparkles swirled around the kitten. A split-second later, the kitten had vanished and an enormous striped tiger had appeared in its place. The tiger turned towards the dog and roared.

Immediately, the dog
pulled up short, its
ears back. Then,
with a frightened
whimper, it
turned tail and
charged away
as fast it could.

Kirsty and Rachel
stared in disbelief, as with
another flash of bright sparkles, the
tiger turned back into a kitten.

The kitten gave
itself a shake,
licked one
paw, and
then padded
off happily
through the grass.

Rachel rubbed her
eyes. "Did you
see what I just
saw?" she asked
wonderingly,
her eyes
still fixed
on the kitten.

Kirsty nodded.
"Yes," she replied.
"That looked like fairy magic!"

Rachel was grinning. "That's exactly
what I thought," she replied. Whenever
she and Kirsty were together, they
always had the most wonderful magical
adventures – and this looked like it
might be the start of another one.

Then Rachel paused. "But…we
haven't seen a fairy!"

Kirsty looked thoughtful. "It is a bit odd, isn't it?" she said. "Let's follow the kitten – maybe it will lead us to a fairy."

The two girls hurried after the small kitten. It seemed to be in no real hurry as it padded along, occasionally pouncing on a daisy, or batting at a blade of grass that was swaying in the breeze.

"Where's it going, do you think?"
Rachel asked in a low voice. "It seems
to be heading right for that fence."

They both watched as the kitten
gambolled merrily towards the wooden
fence. The fence looked far too high for
the kitten to climb over, and yet it
showed no sign of changing direction.

"How is the kitten going to—?"
Kirsty started, but then she broke
off in surprise.

With another glittering
swirl of magic, the kitten
had suddenly shrunk!
It was now the size
of a mouse, small
enough to squeeze
through a tiny hole at
the bottom of the fence.

Kirsty's eyes widened as she watched its little grey tail disappearing through the gap.

"Wow!" Rachel gasped, staring after it. Then she added, "Quick – there's a gate further along the fence. We mustn't lose sight of that kitten!"

Both girls rushed through the gate to see that the kitten was now full-size once more. There was only the tiniest tell-tale trail of magical sparkles glimmering in its wake to show that it had ever been any different.

The kitten twitched its whiskers and bounded towards a fish and chip van. As the girls drew closer, they saw it run purposefully up to a man who was standing at the counter.

"Fish fingers and chips, please," the girls heard him say.

The kitten meowed loudly, and wound itself around the man's legs as the girl behind the counter handed over a plateful of food.

The man chuckled. "Sorry, kitty," he said, sitting down at a nearby bench and spearing a chip on his fork. "This lot's for me, not you."

As the man began tucking into his meal, Kirsty elbowed Rachel in excitement. The kitten's eyes were glowing a brilliant green, and a small cloud of amber sparkles glittered in the air as it looked hopefully up at the man's food. A second later, a fish finger tumbled off the man's plate and landed right at the kitten's feet.

With a happy mew, the kitten
pounced on the fish
finger and began
eating it.

The man
laughed. "It's
your lucky day,
kitty," he said.
"How on earth did
I manage to knock that off the plate?"

Rachel and Kirsty grinned at each
other. Cheeky kitten! They knew very
well that it had used magic to make
the fish finger fall to the ground.

"That was definitely fairy magic!"
Kirsty exclaimed, watching as the
kitten gobbled up the fish finger, gave
its whiskers a quick wash and then
trotted off along a wooded footpath.

"Yes," Rachel agreed. "Something strange is going on. Let's see where the kitten goes now." The girls set off after the kitten again.

They hadn't got far when they heard a scuffling sound in the undergrowth. Suddenly, six green goblins, clutching butterfly nets, jumped out from behind a tree.

"There it is!" shouted one of the goblins, pointing jubilantly at the kitten. "Get it!"

Surprise Attack!

"Goblins!" Kirsty cried in alarm.
"Oh, no!"

At the sight of the goblins, the kitten's fur stood up on end and its tail fluffed up like a bottle-brush. It hissed at the goblins, then turned and ran away from them, towards the girls. With nowhere else to hide, it leapt straight up into Rachel's arms!

"Oh!" Rachel gasped, a little surprised to find herself holding the little bundle of fur. She cuddled the kitten protectively as the goblins approached.

"Give us that kitten!" one of the goblins ordered. A cunning expression crept over his face. "It belongs to Jack Frost, and we've been sent to take it home," he added.

Kirsty and Rachel hesitated. They'd
met Jack Frost's goblins before, many
times, and knew what sneaky creatures
they could be. Could they
really trust them to be
telling the truth?

The kitten gave
a plaintive mew,
and both girls looked
down at it. Its eyes
were shining a brilliant
green again and amber-coloured
sparkles streamed out of its mouth
and swirled around in the air. The
kitten mewed again, but this time the
girls could hear words in its meows.

"Don't believe those goblins," the
kitten declared. "I belong to Katie
the Kitten Fairy, but I'm lost!"

Kirsty's fingers quickly closed over the locket she wore around her neck. She and Rachel had been given matching gold lockets full of fairy dust by the Fairy King and Queen. The fairy dust would magic them straight to Fairyland if they ever needed help – and now seemed like a very good time to use it.

"We don't believe you," Rachel told the goblins as Kirsty threw golden fairy dust all over herself, Rachel and the kitten. "And you're not getting this kitten!"

With angry cries, two of the goblins dropped their butterfly nets and leapt towards the girls, stretching their gnarly green hands out to grab the kitten.

Rachel yelped and tried to dodge out of the way, but luckily, the fairy dust was already working its magic. The girls were swept up into the sky, leaving the goblins to pounce on empty air and topple over together in the grass.

Rachel and Kirsty laughed in relief as they looked down at the goblins and felt the fairy dust whisking them through the air. After a moment, they could no longer see the park below them, just a blur of bright, sparkling colours all around. Rachel held the kitten close in case it was frightened, but it seemed quite used to fairy magic and snuggled up happily in Rachel's arms, its little ears blowing back in the warm, sparkly breeze.

Moments later, the girls floated softly down to the ground. As the magical wind died away, they both smiled to see that they were back in Fairyland.

"We're fairies!" Rachel exclaimed happily, fluttering her delicate gauzy wings.

"And there's the fairy palace and the King and Queen!" Kirsty cheered, waving as King Oberon and Queen Titania approached. Then she frowned.

"They don't look very happy, though," she added.

Rachel watched as the King and Queen drew nearer, followed by a crowd of anxious-looking fairies. Her delight at being back in Fairyland evaporated as she saw how glum they all seemed to be. Something was clearly troubling them. Whatever could be wrong?

Missing Magic Pets

"Hello, Your Majesties," Rachel
said politely, bobbing a little curtsey
with the kitten still in her arms.
"Is everything all right?"

A fairy with long, straight dark
hair, wearing a pale yellow dress,
suddenly caught sight of the kitten
and a happy smile lit up her face.

"You've brought Shimmer back!" she cried. "Oh, thank you, thank you!"

The kitten jumped out of Rachel's

arms at once and scampered over to the pretty fairy who gathered her up for a cuddle, burying her face in Shimmer's soft, silky fur. "Thank you so much," the fairy said, putting Shimmer down and turning to hug Kirsty and Rachel in turn.

"I'm Katie the Kitten Fairy, and I can't tell you how glad I am to see Shimmer back in Fairyland!"

"You're welcome," Rachel said, smiling.
The King and Queen stepped forwards.

"How lovely to see you again, girls,"
the King said warmly. "These are our
Pet Keeper Fairies. You've met Katie,
now here's Bella the Bunny Fairy,
Georgia the Guinea Pig Fairy, Lauren
the Puppy Fairy, Harriet the Hamster
Fairy, Molly the Goldfish Fairy and
Penny the Pony Fairy."

Each fairy stepped forwards in turn
and curtseyed to the girls with a little
smile, but Kirsty couldn't help noticing
that their smiles were rather forlorn.

"So, where are all the other pets?" she
asked curiously.

A sigh came from all the fairies at her
question.

"Jack Frost stole them," the Fairy
Queen told the girls sadly. "He took
them to his ice castle, then sent out
a ransom note. It said that if the Pet
Keeper Fairies couldn't find him a pet
of his own, he would keep all their
magic pets for himself."

"Oh, no!" Kirsty cried out. "He can't
do that!"

"I'm afraid he already has," the King
responded. "And without their magic

pets, the Pet Keeper Fairies can't look after all the pets in the human world."

"The Pet Keeper Fairies are responsible for helping pets who are lost or homeless," the Queen explained. "But they can't do that while their magic pets are missing."

"Well, can't we give Jack Frost another pet, so that he will let the magic pets go free?" Rachel suggested.

The Queen shook her head. "I'm afraid it's not that simple," she sighed. "In Fairyland, the pets *choose* their owners. And no pet has ever chosen Jack Frost."

"I'm not surprised!" Kirsty blurted out
indignantly. Jack Frost was a bad fairy
who was always causing trouble in
Fairyland. No wonder none of the
magic pets wanted to live with him.

The King was gazing
at Shimmer
with a curious
expression on
his face.
"Kirsty, Rachel,
where did you find
Shimmer?" he asked.
"We thought all the
magic pets were locked
away in Jack Frost's ice castle."
"She was in our local park," Kirsty
replied. "Just wandering about as if
she was lost."

The kitten gave a sudden loud meow, as if she was joining in the conversation. Katie listened hard, then nodded. "Shimmer says that the magic pets were all being kept in Jack Frost's castle," she declared. "But they managed to escape and now they're all in the human world."

The Pet Keeper Fairies looked pleased to hear this, but Shimmer was still meowing. Katie listened again, then bit her lip.

"Jack Frost has sent out a gang of goblins to catch them and take them back," she announced anxiously. "Oh, poor little pets!"

A gasp went up from the other Pet Keeper Fairies. The King and Queen looked worried, too.

"We've got to find the pets before the goblins do!" the Queen said, determinedly.

Kirsty and Rachel looked at one another, then both at the same time said, "We'll help!"

Girls on Guard

All the fairies cheered when the girls said they would help.

"Thank you," King Oberon said, smiling. "It's very kind of you to help us once again."

"The magic pets may be hard to find," Queen Titania warned. "In Fairyland, they are tiny, fairy-sized pets, but in the human world, they can be any size they wish. They can also work some fairy magic of their own, so you will have to look very carefully."

Shimmer meowed suddenly and Katie  bent her head to listen. Her face grew serious.

"Shimmer's just told me that a kitten in the human world needs our help," she told the others. "It has no home and Shimmer and I need to find one for it."

She turned to the King and Queen. "May we please go to the rescue?"

The King and Queen both hesitated. "We'd love you to help…" the Queen began slowly.

"But we don't want the goblins to catch Shimmer," the King finished.

"Perhaps we could go with Katie and Shimmer?" Kirsty suggested excitedly. "We could protect them from the goblins."

The King and Queen looked at one another.

Then the Queen nodded. "Very well," she said. "That's very kind. But you must all be careful. You know how cunning the goblins can be."

"We'll be careful," Katie said, her face lighting up. "Let's go!" She waved her wand, and a trail of amber fairy dust flooded out from its tip.

The dust cascaded around Kirsty and
Rachel and, suddenly, Fairyland blurred
before their eyes. A magical wind swept
them up and took them whizzing
through the air with Katie and
Shimmer.

In a rush of colour and light, the girls
found themselves back in their own
world and human-sized once again.

"We're back in the park," Rachel said, looking around. "Watch out for goblins, everyone!"

Katie was still holding Shimmer, and she flew to hide on Kirsty's shoulder while the girls looked around for goblins.

The magic kitten jumped down from Katie's arms and curled up on Kirsty's shoulder. Kirsty could feel his little tail twitching back and forth.

"That tickles," Kirsty giggled, as Shimmer batted playfully at her hair.

"The coast's clear," Rachel said after a few moments of scanning the park. "Let's start looking for a homeless kitten."

"We'll have to search carefully," Katie advised. "If it's frightened it could have hidden itself away."

The four of them set off, listening out for plaintive mewing. Katie flew between the girls at shoulder height, while Shimmer gambolled along beside her in mid-air.  *How fascinating to watch him*, Kirsty thought. Although the tiny kitten was hovering magically in mid-air, he moved just as if he was on the ground – sometimes padding along, occasionally pouncing, and every so often stopping to stalk a floating dandelion seed, or to chase his own fluffy tail. He seemed particularly interested in the bobble holding Rachel's ponytail, which had a couple of pink stars dangling from it. Several times, he leapt up to catch the stars between his tiny paws.

"Come on, Shimmer, we've got work to do," Katie reminded him, fluttering over to scoop him out of Rachel's hair.

"Where could that lost kitten be?"

Suddenly, Shimmer pricked up his
ears and stopped. His little pink nose
turned up and his whiskers twitched
as he sniffed the air. Then he took
a flying leap down to the ground and,
with a bright burst of sparkles, grew to
the size of a normal kitten. He raced
off ahead of the girls towards the
children's playground.

"He's found the kitten," Katie smiled, zooming after her pet. "Come on, girls!"

Rachel and Kirsty ran after Shimmer as he bolted through the grass. Just before he reached the children's playground, he swerved towards a tall elm tree and sat at the bottom, looking upwards.

Kirsty, Rachel and Katie gazed up to see what Shimmer had found. There, on one of the highest branches, huddled against the trunk and looking down at them with big golden eyes, sat a tiny tabby kitten.

Shimmer Has a Plan

"Poor little thing!" Kirsty exclaimed. "It's only a baby!"

A breeze blew through the tree just then, and the tabby kitten pounced on a leaf that was flapping nearby. It almost lost its balance and tumbled out of the tree as it did so.

"Careful, kitty," Katie called up, and the kitten sat down and started washing its paws in a business-like manner.

Shimmer ran a little way up the tree towards the tabby kitten and started meowing. The kitten mewed back eagerly.

"Oh, dear, the kitten climbed the tree to shelter from the wind last night and now it's stuck," Katie translated. "It's too scared to climb back down."

"Shall I climb up and get it?" Rachel offered.

Before Katie could reply, Shimmer started meowing again. The fairy listened, then looked over at the nearby playground. "Good idea, Shimmer," she said, smiling. Then she turned back to the girls. "Thanks for the offer, Rachel, but Shimmer's got someone else in mind for the job," she explained with a grin. She pointed her wand in the direction of the playground. "See that boy in a red shirt at the top of the climbing frame?" she asked.

"The one with black hair?" Kirsty replied.

Katie nodded. "That's the one," she said. "Would you go and ask him if he can help you get the kitten down from the tree?"

"OK," Kirsty agreed, looking puzzled.

"Trust me," Katie said. "It's very

important that it is that boy in particular who rescues this kitten." She winked at the girls, and Shimmer meowed firmly, as if he was agreeing with his fairy owner.

"All right," Rachel laughed. "Come on, Kirsty."

Shimmer immediately shrank back down to fairy pet size, and he and Katie hid in the tree as Rachel and Kirsty ran to the playground. The dark-haired boy had just jumped off the climbing frame as the girls arrived.

"Hello," Kirsty said in a friendly way. "I'm Kirsty and this is Rachel. Could you help us rescue a kitten that's stuck up a tree?"

"We saw how good you are at climbing," Rachel explained, "so we wondered if you could climb up the tree and get him down?"

"Sure," the boy replied eagerly. "I love cats. Where is he?"

The girls pointed out the elm tree and the boy, whose name was James, called over to tell his dad where he was going, then followed Kirsty and Rachel to the tree.

James looked up at the kitten. "Don't worry, little kitten, I'll have you down in two minutes," he called, and began to climb.

Kirsty and Rachel watched as he clambered higher. Then, just as he was about to reach the branch that the tabby kitten was on, the kitten jumped down onto his shoulder, and butted its head gently against James's cheek.

Kirsty blinked as a haze of amber sparkles seemed to surround James and the kitten. She looked at Rachel and they grinned knowingly at each other: more Pet Fairy magic!

James carefully carried the tabby kitten all the way back down to the ground. "It's so tiny," he marvelled, stroking it gently. "I wonder where it lives."

"It doesn't have a collar or a name-tag," Kirsty said. "It looks like a stray."

"Here comes my dad," James said, as a tall, dark-haired man strolled over. "Dad, look! We've found a lost kitten!"

His eyes brightened suddenly. "Hey, Dad, can we keep it?"

James's dad smiled. "Funnily enough, your mum and I have been talking about getting you a pet," he said. "But we can't just take this one without checking it doesn't belong to somebody else." He looked around to see if the kitten's owner was somewhere in the park.

"We've been here for a while," Kirsty said politely. "And nobody seems to be looking for it."

"Please!" James said quickly, seeing his dad hesitate. "We can take it home with us, and phone the animal shelter from our house." He stroked it again. "Oh, it's purring, Dad. It likes me, see?"

James's dad ruffled his son's hair. "Very

well," he said. "And if everything
checks out, and nobody's reported it
missing, then I think you can keep it."

"Yay!" cheered James, beaming from
ear to ear. He tickled the tabby kitten
under its chin, and the kitten purred
even louder. "Do you think 'Dusty'
might be a good name?" James
wondered aloud.

Rachel nudged Kirsty; she had spotted a few last flecks of fairy dust twinkling in the air around James and the kitten. "Oh, Dusty would be a wonderful name," she said, trying not to giggle.

"Well, then, Dusty," James's dad said, stroking the kitten himself. "We'd better take you home, hadn't we?"

Grasping Goblins

The girls watched as James walked away happily with his dad and his new kitten.

"A job well done," Katie sighed, as she emerged from her hiding place in the tree. "Good work, girls! Dusty and James will be very happy together."

Shimmer scampered along a branch,

purring loudly as if he agreed, and the
girls laughed.

"Fairy magic is fantastic!" Rachel said
with a smile, watching as Shimmer
sniffed a beetle on a leaf
and gave a tiny,
fairy-sized sneeze.
Just then, Kirsty
heard a rustling
sound from a little
higher up in the
tree. She looked up to
see a goblin – and then
another – and then another! She gasped
as she realised that there was a whole
chain of grinning goblins hanging
down from one branch of the tree.
The goblin lowest down was dangling
just above the branch where Shimmer

was perched – and he was reaching
out to grab the magic kitten!

"No, you don't!" cried Kirsty,
scooping up Shimmer, just in time.

"Give it here!" the goblin growled,
making a lunge for the kitten.

Shimmer meowed in alarm as the goblin's fingers came within a whisker of him. But the goblin had reached out too far, and the other goblins couldn't hold him. They all tumbled to the ground, landing in a great green heap of tangled arms and legs.

"Ouch! You're squashing me!"
grumbled one goblin.

"Get off!" moaned another.

Katie grinned at the girls. "Come on,
let's go while we have the chance,"
she said.

Kirsty held out her hands and let
Shimmer run happily
back to Katie
as they all walked
away from the
pile of grumpy
goblins. "I don't
think Jack Frost
will be pleased
when they come
back empty-handed,"
she said, glancing back over her
shoulder to see them still bickering.

"No," Katie agreed. She gave
a sudden shiver. "He's sure to send
them straight back out again in search
of another pet." She cuddled her kitten
tightly at the thought. "Let's get you
safely back to Fairyland,
Shimmer," she said in
her sweet silvery voice.
"Goodbye girls – and
thank you
for everything."
Katie hugged
the girls in turn,
and then Shimmer
nuzzled his tiny nose
against each of their faces.
"Goodbye, little Shimmer," Kirsty
said, giggling as his fur tickled her nose.
"It's been lovely to meet you."

"Tell the other Pet Keeper Fairies
that we'll keep looking for
the other lost magic
pets," Rachel added,
blowing Katie
and Shimmer
one last kiss.

"We will,"
Katie promised.
"Goodbye
now!" She
tucked Shimmer
carefully under
one arm, then
waved her wand.

A shower of
amber-coloured lights
twinkled around the fairy and her
magic pet, and then they were gone.

Rachel and Kirsty smiled at each other and began to head for home. After all the excitement, they both felt quite hungry. "I'm so pleased we found a nice home for Dusty," Rachel said happily. "Everything worked out perfectly."

Kirsty slipped her arm through Rachel's as they neared the park gates.

"I can't wait to find another of the lost fairy pets," she said excitedly, and grinned at her friend. "It looks like we're going to have another brilliant fairy holiday together!"

The Pet Keeper Fairies

Katie the Kitten Fairy has got
her pet back. Now Rachel
and Kirsty must help

Bella the Bunny Fairy

Win a Rainbow Magic
Sparkly T-Shirt and Goody Bag!

In every book in the Rainbow Magic Pet Keeper Fairies series (books 29-35) there is a hidden picture of a collar with a secret letter in it. Find all seven letters and re-arrange them to make a special Fairyland word, then send it to us. Each month we will put the entries into a draw and select one winner to receive a Rainbow Magic Sparkly T-shirt and Goody Bag!

Send your entry on a postcard to Rainbow Magic Pet Keeper Competition, Orchard Books, 338 Euston Road, London NW1 3BH. Australian readers should write to Hachette Children's Books, Level 17/207 Kent Street, Sydney, NSW 2000.
Don't forget to include your name and address.
Only one entry per child. Final draw: 30th April 2007.

Don't miss...
Kylie the Carnival Fairy

Kylie the Carnival Fairy needs Kirsty's and Rachel's help! Jack Frost has stolen the three magic hats that make the Sunnydays Carnival so much fun, and the girls have to get them back...

1-84616-175-4

Have you checked out the

website at:

www.rainbowmagic.co.uk

There are games, activities and fun things to do, as well as news and information about Rainbow Magic and all of the fairies.

by Daisy Meadows

The Jewel Fairies

The Pet Keeper Fairies

All priced at £3.99. *Holly the Christmas Fairy, Summer the Holiday Fairy,
Stella the Star Fairy* and *Kylie the Carnival Fairy* are priced at £4.99.
The Rainbow Magic Treasury is priced at £12.99.
Rainbow Magic books are available from all good bookshops, or can be ordered
direct from the publisher: Orchard Books, PO BOX 29, Douglas IM99 1BQ
Credit card orders please telephone 01624 836000
or fax 01624 837033 or visit our Internet site: www.wattspub.co.uk
or e-mail: bookshop@enterprise.net for details.

To order please quote title, author and ISBN and your full name and address.
Cheques and postal orders should be made payable to 'Bookpost plc.'
Postage and packing is FREE within the UK
(overseas customers should add £2.00 per book).
Prices and availability are subject to change.

Look out for the Fun Day Fairies!

MEGAN THE MONDAY FAIRY
1-84616-188-6

TALLULAH THE TUESDAY FAIRY
1-84616-189-4

WILLOW THE WEDNESDAY FAIRY
1-84616-190-8

THEA THE THURSDAY FAIRY
1-84616-191-6

FREYA THE FRIDAY FAIRY
1-84616-192-4

SIENNA THE SATURDAY FAIRY
1-84616-193-2

SARAH THE SUNDAY FAIRY
1-84616-194-0

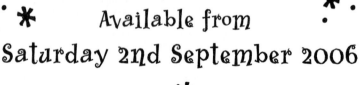

Available from
Saturday 2nd September 2006